Harry Kitten
and
Tucker Mouse

Meet Harry Kitten and Tucker Mouse. No one would ever dream that a cat and mouse could become friends, but that doesn't stop Harry and Tucker. All they have is each other. Together, they begin an exciting adventure throughout New York, searching for a home they can call their own. But the two friends run into troublesome times in their journey around town. Is all hope lost? Where will they turn to next?

"A splendid prequel to the famous *The Cricket in Times Square* . . . Harry, benign and kindly, and Tucker, energetic and acquisitive, are superb examples of the attraction of opposites and the strength and comfort of friendship."—*The Horn Book*

"The characters of these quintessential New Yorkers are as vibrant and joyful as they ever were. . . . Wonderfully expressive black-and-white illustrations."—*Publishers Weekly*

LEXILE 600L

For Pat Saffron
and I only wish that
this slender book were as big as
the bond that binds me
to her
G.S.

SQUARE
FISH

An imprint of Macmillan Publishing Group, LLC

HARRY KITTEN AND TUCKER MOUSE. Text copyright © 1986 by George Selden.
Pictures copyright © 1986 by Garth Williams. Cover line art © 1986 by Garth Williams.
Cover color art © 1986 by Richard Egielski. All rights reserved.
Printed in the United States of America by
LSC Communications, Harrisonburg, Virginia. For information,
address Square Fish, 175 Fifth Avenue, New York, NY 10010.

Square Fish and the Square Fish logo are trademarks of Macmillan and are used by
Farrar Straus Giroux under license from Macmillan.

Library of Congress catalog card number: 83-16530
ISBN 978-0-312-58248-7

Originally published in the United States by Farrar Straus Giroux
Square Fish logo designed by Filomena Tuosto
First Square Fish Edition: 2009

20 19 18
mackids.com

Harry Kitten
and
Tucker Mouse

GEORGE SELDEN

PICTURES BY

GARTH WILLIAMS

SQUARE
FISH

FARRAR STRAUS GIROUX
NEW YORK

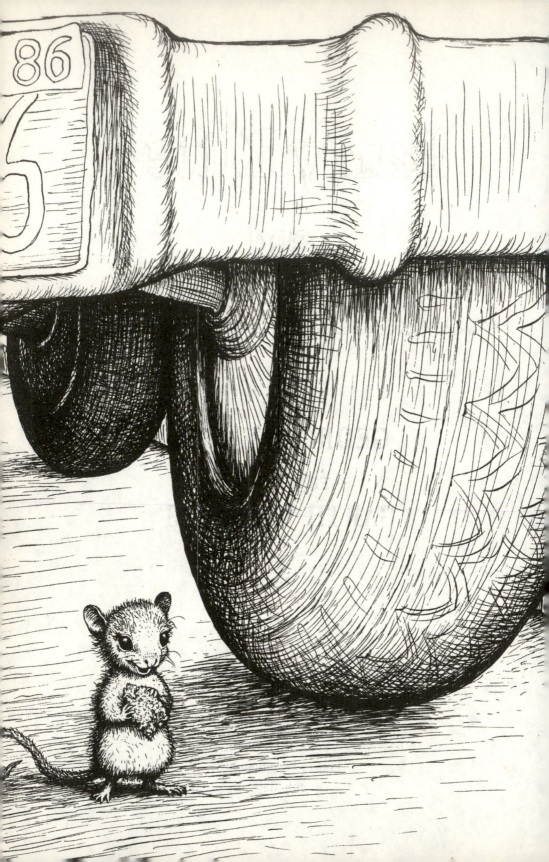

"At least I could have a name!" the tiny mouse said to himself.

He was picking his way, very carefully, along the gutter of Tenth Avenue in New York City. *Whssht!*—just like that, he'd dart from under one parked car to the dark dirty safety beneath another. For this young little mouse had found that the human beings didn't like him much. Some of those two-legged creatures, who thought they owned the whole city, called him a rat—which he definitely was *not*!—when they saw him. And some called him a rodent. And one just said, "Yeck!"—which sounded most unkind of all.

"But at least I can have a name," the mouse said, as

he paused to nibble the crust of a cheese sandwich that one of the human beings had thrown away. He wished there had been more cheese and less crust. "My own name." He quickly hid behind a tire, as a threatening leather boot came near.

"I could be Hamlet. Hamlet Mouse." The night before, in the theater district, the young mouse had heard two human beings, very well dressed, say that they were going to a show called *Hamlet*. "But I don't like 'Hamlet,'" the mouse said to himself. "It sounds too much like a little pig."

There was another possibility. Godzilla Mouse. Two teenage boys were going to a horror movie and the mouse had overheard them talking. "Godzilla Mouse—?"

"It just isn't me," he decided.

But who was he? If he didn't have a name, he wouldn't be anyone. For a name makes a person very special. He is *himself*—and no one else.

A group of young girls walked by the car under which the mouse was hiding.

These laughing young girls—one of them had soft fuzzy hair and a high sweet voice—reminded the mouse of the very first thing that he could remember. That was a nest, made of scraps of cloth, and thrown-away Kleenexes, and other comfortable, cozy odds and ends. And there also was a soft warm furry weight—the word "Mother" rang in his ears—that tried to protect him from pounding shovels, and nasty words, and the threat of death. There were men in uniforms, sanitation workers. And he ran.

He'd run, the young mouse had, and *still* was running.

Since then, there'd been no warmth, no weight, no comforting covering. There had only been darting from one parked car—a temporary refuge—to another.

"But I have to have a *name*!" the mouse said. "So even if I do get tromped on—at least I'll know who's being squashed!"

The motor of the car he was under started up with a roar. The mouse jumped aside.

His jump landed him very near those girls. And in order not to frighten them, because young girls and young mice sometimes do not get along, he hid between two garbage cans. Not a very nice place, to be sure—but the little mouse had been in worse. And also, he was near enough to hear the girls talking, a rippling, happy sound.

"I'm hungry," said one.

"So'm I," said another.

"Well, this is the best bakery on Tenth Avenue," said a third girl. "Merry Tucker's Home-Baked Goods. Does

anyone feel like a glazed doughnut or a raspberry tart? They're to *die* over, they're so good!"

The girls twittered their excitement. And went into the bakery.

And oh!—a glazed doughnut! A raspberry tart! The little mouse—whose mouth was now watering—could have died over either one. But something even more interesting echoed in his ears. *Merry Tucker's Home-Baked Goods.*

He felt there was something special in those words. A name!

"It can't be Merry," he said to himself. "Sounds too

11

much like Mary." And if you were going to grow up and be a "he" mouse—well, a name like Mary would just not do.

But Tucker—he mused and repeated the name. "Tucker Mouse." It sounded quite original. Not ordinary like Tom, or Joe, or Bill. "*Tucker* Mouse!" he shouted. "That's me."

The name tasted more sweet and more strong in his mouth than even a raspberry tart.

So, armed with his name, the mouse marched—through the gutter, it's true—but he marched down Tenth Avenue. His name—Tucker Mouse—which he'd looked for so long gave him strength, courage—gave him life!

Tucker Mouse skittered after the girls, darting close to the buildings that lined the street. He was hoping that one of the girls might drop a little piece of pastry. But, sadly, they all liked tarts and doughnuts as much as he did, and smacking their lips, which made it worse, not one of them dropped a single crumb.

Then up ahead he saw what he feared most of all in the world: a garbage truck—and all around it, sanitation workers scooping up trash from the sidewalk. Tucker Mouse knew that the uniformed men thought he was trash, too. He felt lonely and afraid again.

And tired. So tired. He had to find a place to rest. A narrow, dark alley opened between a tenement and a dry cleaner's. As Tucker was scooting in, he happened to see a small copper coin on the sidewalk. Instinctively, he snatched it up in his two front paws—then vanished into the sheltering dark.

"A penny!" he exclaimed out loud—quite proud that he'd found it, and saved it.

"The human beings think pennies are good luck," said a voice behind him.

Tucker whirled around. In the dark behind him, nibbling a crust—the remains of a sandwich—he saw a kitten. His first thought was: Poor guy! He's as starved

15

as I am. But then he remembered: I am a *mouse*—and this is a kitten, who will very likely become a *cat*.

"Ya wanna fight?" he demanded.

"Why?" The kitten put down his crust, and simply asked, "Why?"

"Well—well—" Tucker Mouse was flustered. "It's just that—well—cats and mice *fight*. That's all."

"But why?" the kitten continued to question. "I was starving to death before I found this pitiful piece of sandwich. Some overfed human being missed that

garbage can, so *I* got to eat. And you don't look too beefy yourself. So why make life worse for each other by fighting?"

Tucker Mouse was somewhat taken aback. He hadn't expected such reasonable talk from a skinny kitten sitting next to a trash can and a decaying pumpkin.

"But—what do we do if we *don't* fight?" asked Tucker.

"Mmm—" The kitten purred softly, like a philosopher. "We could just be friends—"

"*What—?*"

"Not so loud. The human beings are all around."

Tucker nodded ruefully: they were surrounded.

"I know that it's unusual," said the kitten. "At least, I know it's supposed to be. But this is New York! And all the rules are broken here. For the best, I hope. We might even set a precedent—"

"What's a precedent?"

"It's a new way of thinking," said the kitten. "And a new way of feeling, too."

"You promise not to eat me?"

"I will never be *that* hungry." The kitten patted the small mouse's head. "And even if I was—I couldn't. My teeth aren't big enough. Yet."

"Mmm—" The mouse had to think about that. "For a mouse to trust a cat—"

"You've got to trust somebody—sooner or later," the kitten declared. "Why not try me?"

"Well—okay. For a while. But I'm keeping an eye on those teeth!"

Tucker sighed and looked down the alley, where some sanitation workers were doing their job. For a moment he even wished them well. They have problems, too, he thought to himself—but I hope that I am not one of them.

"You want some sandwich?"

Tucker Mouse said nothing.

"Come on," urged the kitten. "It's ham-and-cheese. Mice like cheese—"

19

"Ohhh!" Tucker groaned with delight.

"Then just you munch on this piece. See? There is ham and *also* cheese on this crust."

"I *am* sort of hungry—" admitted Tucker. "But it isn't a raspberry tart."

"Well, listen to the mousiekins!" The kitten purred. "Next time I'll try to supply—"

"Don't you *dare* call me mousiekins!"

"—beef steak. Or corned beef."

"Oh, can I have a bite?" said the mouse. "I'm so *hungry*! You can't believe—"

"It's all yours," said the kitten. "I'm full."

"Full?" The thought of being full of food had never occurred to the mouse before.

"Munch out!" said the kitten.

And Tucker munched.

Between mouthfuls—for there's more to a crust than a human being might think—he asked, "What's your name?"

And then, before the kitten could answer, he explained, between munches, why his name was Tucker.

"Why, that's very much like—it's exactly what happened to me!" said the kitten. And friendship, like a frail tree, grew between them.

"I, too," said the kitten, "was hiding from everybody. I wanted to be invisible—" The kitten sighed. "Although I had always felt I was—well, you know—special."

"Me, too," said Tucker.

20

"But then two kids walked by." The kitten's voice brightened. "And one had an arm around the other's shoulders—these two nice guys were just talking like friends." The kitten purred at the memory. "And then the one with scraggly blond hair said, 'Harry—you're a *character*!' "

The kitten's eyes blazed at the memory. " 'Harry—you're a character!' the kid said. So I knew that was my name," said the kitten, "since I've always wanted to be a character. And a *character*'s name is Harry!"

The kitten fell silent. Except for a purr, which sounded to Tucker's attentive ears like loyalty and, maybe, trust.

"So I'm Harry," said the kitten.

"And I am Tucker," said the mouse.

A thoughtful silence grew long, and then longer, between them. But outside the private silence they shared were taxis honking, huge trucks roaring—the din and danger of New York.

"So where do we go from here?" asked the mouse, with a tremble in his voice that he tried hard to hide.

Harry thought a moment and then exclaimed: "Oh, I know where! There's a great big building—and it must have *lots* and *lots* of cellars—where we'd be safe. Follow me." He began to creep warily down the street. It was evening now, and he and his friend could slip through the failing light like ghosts.

"Wait! Wait!" shouted Tucker. "I have to hide my penny. When I can, I'm going to come back and get it."

There was a Cadillac nearby, and the mouse thought of shoving it under one wheel. It had been parked there a very long time—the meter said so. But the little mouse reconsidered. If it had been there so long, the police would probably be coming soon to drag it away to the place where cars went to jail until their owners came to claim them.

"Every mouse should have his Life Savings. And this penny is the beginning of mine."

He decided, finally, and after much scuttling back and forth, that it just might be safe wedged between two bricks in the tenement wall that faced the alley. "Now don't let me forget where I've put it."

"I have a suspicion you'll *never* forget," said the kitten.

By now, he'd begun to form an idea of his friend's character. It was—no, not "greedy"—but rather, "acquisitive." Which is much the same thing, but in much nicer terms.

"I am ready," Tucker Mouse announced. "Now where?"

"To the deep and mysterious lower levels of the greatest building in all the world," said the kitten. "The fantastic and fabulous Empire State Building!"

"Oh," mumbled Tucker. "I never heard of it."

Harry made a face—which looked like pity (or maybe disbelief). "Even the meekest mouse," he said, "must surely have heard of the Empire State."

"Well, I haven't," said Tucker. "So show me."

An hour's scurrying, hurrying, worrying—then it rose above them: beautiful and unbelievable.

"They really do know something," said Tucker. "The human beings." He looked up, up. "Just look at that!"

"Let's see what's underground," said Harry Kitten. "I've heard about those cellars ever since I can remember."

"And when is that?" asked Tucker, with a hush in his voice.

"I don't know," said Harry. "The first thing—the really very first thing—I remember is shivering, last month, in a pipe made of iron. There was some cat there —little, like me, with black-and-white fur. Then I forget. But maybe I have brothers and sisters somewhere."

"Show me the building," said Tucker Mouse. He

coughed, because Harry seemed to be dreaming and sad, and Tucker had to interrupt. "And tell me all about, and show me, all the fantastic, fabulous cellars. Underground. Please? Harry? Even if they're scary."

"Okay," said Harry. His voice was still dull. "But I don't know about the lower levels."

"Come on," said Tucker. "Let's adventure."

"We have to go down, and down, and down," said Harry.

The kitten and the mouse prowled carefully around the huge building. And in back they found a freight elevator on the street level that hadn't completely closed. Like two furry, quick blinks—and they almost *were* invisible—they dashed through.

It was eight o'clock, and most of the weary human beings had, gratefully, gone home.

"We're in luck," said Harry. "We can prowl at our leisure."

They jumped down to the floor below. A dark passageway, barely lit by a series of weak white bulbs, stretched endlessly ahead of them.

"We may need a hunk of that stuff, luck," said Tucker, staring into the gloom. "I wish I had my penny."

"Oh, we'll be lucky!" said Harry jauntily. "As you said before: let's do some exploring. Adventuring!"

The stairways—some marked EMERGENCY EXIT—the airshafts, the endless, endless corridors—no one can describe the lower levels of the Empire State Building.

At one point, outside a closed elevator door, Tucker had to stand on Harry's shoulders—even with the help of a nearby ladder—to push the button with an arrow on it that pointed down.

"I suppose that's us," said the mouse, as he weaved and wobbled dangerously, and finally managed to push that button. "There."

The door opened—they entered—nobody there—and the elevator began to descend. And descend. And *descend*!

"Harry—we are coming out in *China*."

"No, we're not. Just wait." The kitten sounded very sure—for someone who wasn't all that sure. At last the elevator stopped. The door opened. Out they ran. "You see, mousiekins—"

"I have asked you not—"

"—the lowest level. That's what the elevator button says. We're here. And get off my shoulders, by the way."

"The lowest level," mused Tucker Mouse. "To think that it should come to this."

"Fewer human beings to worry us." Harry offered his jaunty suggestion as hope. "Anyway—we're here."

Here? Here was a tunnel with white tiles for a floor, and white tiles for a ceiling, and also white tiles for walls. *Here*, in fact, was *all* white tiles—and not even a sanitation inspector in sight.

"There is absolutely no one around," the kitten went on.

"So I've noticed," said Tucker, eyeing the icy-white canyon they were in. "A *ghost* would make this place feel alive."

"Now, now—"

"Now *what?*" squeaked Tucker Mouse. "We are on the bottomest level. And it feels—and it looks—like Dead Man's Gulch."

"At the very worst," said Harry, "there is nobody
here—"

"That's just it! *Nobody*."

"—who would want to do us harm."

28

"At this point," said Tucker, "the chance of a little harm might be quite exciting."

"Shall we take the elevator back up to level four?" asked Harry. "There may be janitors there."

"Let's try it here for a while," said Tucker.

For hours these two—a kitten who wanted to seem very brave and a mouse who was afraid to admit he was scared —roamed through the labyrinth that lies far beneath the Empire State Building.

Now and then they caught sight of men in uniform, the caretakers of the building, who roamed about doing odd jobs—for a building is like a living thing: it needs to be taken care of. That night, there were only a few lonely men. And they were quite easy to avoid.

The solitude, however, the silence and the isolation— they were not so easy to avoid. But still—no one even knew the kitten and the mouse were there.

Food was no problem. The caretakers were very careless. They left little bits of lunches around. A shred of lettuce—a bit of bread—now and then a glob of yogurt in a container.

But lettuce and bread—and even the dregs of old milk shakes—are really very dull. If you have too much of them.

"I'd love a hunk of cheese," said Tucker.

"Umm," purred Harry. "Roast beef for me."

The next day came up above. Of course, deep down, they couldn't tell day from night. Tucker looked around, scratched one ear, and said, "Harry, have we been in this particular corridor before?"

"I don't know," said Harry. "They all look alike."

"Precisely!" said Tucker. "That means we are—"

"Don't say it!"

"—*lost*!"

Neither said a word . . .

Then Tucker remembered. "You know—Tenth Avenue wasn't dull. It was very lively, in fact."

"Especially when the sanitation workers were trying to bash you with shovels," said Harry.

"We've got to get out of here!" shouted Tucker. "I'm going out of my mind!"

"I agree," said Harry, sighing. "The Empire State Building—beautiful as it is—is not the place for us."

"But we're lost," shrieked Tucker. "And there's no ladder here. Even if we could find an elevator."

There is no more pitiful sight than a young mouse wringing his paws.

"Now, just you wait," said Harry Kitten. And for a kitten, he had learned to speak with a bit of authority. "I have seen something you have *not!*"

"You've seen?" Tucker Mouse talked loudest. But Harry only purred the truth. "What? *What?*"

"I have seen a chalk mark on the wall." Harry, with one paw, pointed to a slender line of chalk that ran along one wall. "We are not the only souls who've been alone down here. One human being also was afraid to get lost. And he'll show us the way out."

"He will?" Tucker couldn't believe his ears.

"He was scared, too. But he had a piece of chalk. And if we follow the line he made—to find his way out—"

"Let's go," yelled Tucker. "Whoever you are—you human being—please save us, too, who are only animals!"

And the chalk line, scribbled on the wall, led Tucker and Harry, as it had that man, to the street.

(The man's name was Matthew. He lived in Queens—which is part of New York—and he had four sons. And the night he drew the chalk line—so he'd know where he had been already—that night was Halloween. And he was on duty—a lucky accident, two years later, for a kitten and a mouse.)

"The street!" said Tucker Mouse and sighed. "Oh, the street."

He was just about to feel relieved when "Watch out!" warned Harry. "Here comes a garbage truck."

"We've got to run—"

"Follow me!" shouted Tucker.

"Follow *you*?"

"I've got brains, too! Maybe little ones—but when I was on Tenth Avenue, just trying to stay alive, I heard some kids say they were going down to the docks to get a suntan."

"The docks?" puffed Harry. He had to run to keep up with his friend. "With all those ocean liners?"

"Not *those* docks," said Tucker. "Down in the lower part of New York there are old, abandoned piers, where people get suntans. If they take their shirt off."

"Old, abandoned piers—"

"Yes. Very run-down. So, safe for us."

"Mmm!" Harry Kitten choked as he ran. "I don't quite like the sound of that."

Furtively, in the late afternoon, the kitten and the mouse made their way to the docks.

And if Harry Kitten didn't like those words—"old, abandoned piers"—he liked the old, abandoned piers themselves much less.

Yet it was sunset, and even in their dangerous ruins the docks, the decaying piers of New York, seemed

almost beautiful. Red and orange light illumined the fallen roofs, the leaning walls. And the everlasting sun —in the west—seemed to bless the place. Behind the two friends, as they sat on the pier, the lights of New York

were flickering on. They, too, as they danced on the great flowing river, seemed like a blessing.

But *nothing* blessed the inhabitants of those piers.

"There are rats here," whispered Tucker.

"Well, you're a—"

"I am a *rodent*, I guess. Not a rat! Not me!" He sleeked down his fur. And gave Harry an appealing smile. "We mice have style." Then he growled ferociously. "And rats have *none*. No style. No niceness. No nothing. The *bums*!"

Tucker looked around. "There are human beings here, too. Look at that guy lying over there, asleep."

"Poor soul," murmured Harry. "I hate to see a human

being so down on his luck. They have to find a place of their own, too."

"I agree." Tucker nodded sympathetically. "I also hate to think of a certain kitten I know—and also a mouse —who are so far down on *their* luck that they have to live here. *Yeck!*"

The *"yeck"* burst out because a frantic cockroach— heaven knows where he was going—had just dashed across Tucker's left paw.

"We'll stay here tonight, and then—*watch out!*"

A crunching, tearing sound came from the ceiling of the pier where they were. Harry yanked Tucker Mouse aside—and a huge chunk of plaster fell just where they'd been sitting.

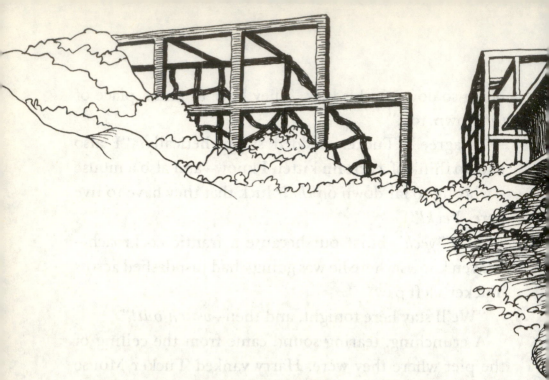

"If we live through the night," said Tucker, wiping plaster dust off his fur.

"Over here," said Harry. A huge girder had fallen from the roof. There was an open space beneath it. "Get under here. Then, even if more of the roof comes down, we'll be safe."

The two animals crawled beneath the beams.

"Safe," said Tucker. "I've about given up on being safe. Even those kids, with their nice suntans, will probably throw rocks at us tomorrow."

"Well, don't give up on being safe. Rocks and falling beams or not," said Harry. He curled up, and in a few minutes a whizzing, purring, zizzing sound told Tucker that he was asleep.

And after fifteen minutes, so was the mouse. His first dream was all about cheeseburgers.

Next morning, at the very same moment, the two woke up—as if the clocks inside their heads were exactly the same. They were that close.

Dawn gloried over the east. The sight made the great buildings of Manhattan look as if they were dreams. Such great dreams!

"I'm hungry." Tucker yawned.

"We've got no *food*."

"Oh," Tucker admitted. "Then, what now—"

"I don't know."

And for the first time Tucker heard, not a whimper, but a fearful tone in Harry's voice.

"Come on, Harry," said Tucker Mouse. "If we have to go on looking—we go!"

All that day and night—what with hurrying, scurrying, worrying—the mouse and the kitten made their way uptown. It meant hiding behind fireplugs, in alleys, under cars. And *so* like the old lonely life it was!

The next morning, just at first light—gold streamed from the east—Harry said, "I see green! Look!"

Ahead of them were trees, shrubs, clipped hedges, aglow in the dawn.

"We have to rest here," said Harry.

Heaving sighs of relief and weariness, Harry Kitten and Tucker Mouse crept under an iron fence, through a hedge, and fell asleep.

They woke up together, and on the dot, as usual.

"Just look at these lovely bushes—those trees," said Harry. "Why, it's a protected little park!"

"Protected from *what*?" asked Tucker, who had noticed that, as well as the barred fence around the park, there was a gate. And it was locked. Only the people who lived nearby had a key to get in.

"Oh, you ask so many questions," said Harry.

"I repeat—if this part of New York is so nice—protected from *what*?"

"Oh—from hoodlums and beggars and troublemakers. And also, I would guess, from horrible dogs who aren't on leashes!"

"And from homeless kittens and mice, too, maybe? A park this well kept could make even me feel like a hoodlum."

"I am trying to find us a place to live—"

"All right. Okay. So we'll give it a try. At least it beats the docks."

So, for a while, one kitten and one mouse lived quietly in Gramercy Park. For that's what it was called. *Very* quietly! Because this park in the heart of New York City seemed to have a discreet sort of upper-class hush about it. Not that there weren't children, or older people, just sitting in the sun, but everyone was—

"They're so polite!" said Tucker.

"You'd rather have rats?" asked Harry, who was munching slowly, to make it last, on half a roast-beef sandwich. The meat was perfectly cooked, too: not too rare, but not too well done. It must have come from a very expensive delicatessen. Harry could not imagine how half a roast-beef sandwich could have been dropped and forgotten in Gramercy Park.

"No, I don't want rats," said Tucker Mouse. "But I wouldn't mind a little *action*! Now, give me a chomp on that roast beef." He gobbled furiously.

"Your manners—my word!" Harry murmured disapprovingly.

Tucker almost choked. "Will you listen to King Kitten here! You improve your manners a little bit more —and lick your fur three times a day—with a little luck, you could get adopted by one of those old women who come here and knit all afternoon. Would you like that, kittykins?"

Harry didn't reply.

Yet Gramercy Park was a beautiful place. Tucker couldn't deny it. There were well-tended trees; there were flowers of all different colors: it was as if an overripe rainbow had burst and scattered its seeds over Gramercy Park. The lawn was clipped as neat and nice as a new haircut. Clean benches were set here and there. And also, all around the square, there were lovely old buildings, town houses. But there also was that high iron fence. (Of course, animals could get in through the bars —but even the animals, and especially the squirrels, had exquisite manners.)

So Tucker and Harry, whose manners were not that exquisite or refined, had just slipped through the bars and found themselves in a very well mannered paradise.

What little creatures were living there—a few well-bred insects, especially—were all of a very high class. One

43

praying mantis even nodded to Tucker—and that had never happened before. Indeed, it was the very first time in New York—and perhaps anywhere—that a praying mantis had nodded cordially to a mouse.

"This is heaven," said Tucker. "I got smiled at by a bug!"

But heaven—and would anyone believe this?—even heaven itself, for a mouse, has its disadvantages. A mouse gets nervous. Especially when he almost gets run over by a baby carriage.

One afternoon, a wee bit bored by nothing but leisure, and the idle beauty of Gramercy Park, Tucker Mouse ventured out on the sidewalk, just for a change,

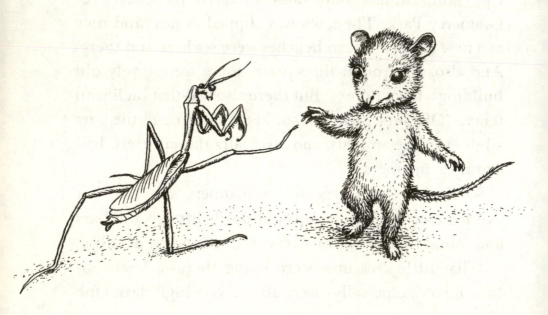

and he almost got squashed by a lovely yellow baby carriage which was being wheeled by a nurse in a starched
white uniform. The nurse herself looked quite starched,
too.

"Harry," said Tucker, when he had returned to the rhododendron bush they were living under, "which would you prefer: to be mashed by a nurse in a stiff uniform or by a bum on the docks?"

"*What?*" asked Harry.

"Or how would you like a life in the fantastic and fabulous corridors—lowest level—of the Empire State Building?"

"Have you gone crazy?" asked Harry.

"Very nearly," said Tucker.

Harry sighed. "And I thought I'd found you happiness."

"Happiness is fine," said Tucker. "But I've got to have some *action*, too. I mean—apart from baby carriages and flowers that never cease to bloom."

Harry lay down, and didn't purr—he sort of moaned. "Docks, skyscrapers—what do you want?"

"I want life, excitement!" shouted Tucker.

"Oh, excitement, life," mused Harry Kitten. "Where is it?"

And then his eyes changed. A glitter, an almost challenging glitter, came into them.

"Harry, stop that," said Tucker. "You don't need to go goofy—"

"Mmm," Harry purred. "Yes, life. And I *know* where it is."

"Where?" squeaked Tucker, who was sounding more like a kitten himself now.

"Times Square!" shouted Harry, although his voice cracked. "The crossroads of the whole city!"

"I'm not sure I'm up to that," whimpered Tucker.

"You'd better be," commanded this little furry kitten, Harry Kitten, who sounded now more like Harry Cat.

"Is it dangerous?" asked Tucker Mouse, wringing his paws again.

"You bet," said Harry Cat.

"Tell me about it," pleaded Tucker Mouse.

"In the very center of the very greatest city, in the very greatest country there is—there is—Times Square! The Heart of the World!"

"Harry, you are frightening me."

"There are subways—trains that run underground— there are candy stores, and hamburger joints—and most of all, there are hurrying, rushing human beings."

"I'm not so keen on them," said Tucker.

"Don't worry—they won't even notice you."

"Well, a little bit of notice," said Tucker, "would not be *too* offensive."

"And there are—I know this, because when I prowled Times Square, I saw pipes and I saw niches, and I saw places to hide."

"But the people, Harry—the human beings—you don't think they'd hound us out?"

Harry shook his head. "They're too much concerned with themselves. If we just keep out of the way of all the life that goes on there."

"Keeping out of the way of life," said Tucker. "Is that a way of life?"

Harry started to laugh. But quickly he stopped. For he saw that some moisture was dribbling down Tucker's furry cheeks.

"We have no place to live," moaned Tucker in a choked voice. "And nobody wants us."

"Now, just a minute!" Harry laid a paw on his small friend's back. "In the first place, we want each other—so

that takes care of that. And in the second, you will like Times Square."

"Well, Harry, if you do—I might like it, too." Tucker's whiskers—very small—were absolutely dripping now.

A curious thing then took place: a kitten wiped a mouse's eyes. Neither one said a word. And the brush of those paws across those wet cheeks was the strangest touch, the most wonderful in all the world.

"Shall we give it a try?" asked Harry quietly.

"I guess so." Tucker sniffed a little. "If you say so, Harry."

And again there began the scuttle and struggle through the streets of New York. It was raining now, too. The kind of dull drizzle that everyone hates. Gray light hushed all the harsh silhouettes of the dangerous city.

But that was fortunate, on this special day. For a gray mouse and a kitten whose fur hadn't quite decided its color could pass almost unseen through the equally gray streets of the city.

The people in Times Square—when Tucker and Harry reached it, safe—were far too busy avoiding the drizzle to notice two shivering little creatures.

"We're in luck," whispered Harry.

"So this is luck," mused Tucker Mouse, as a man with a blaring radio passed by. "That penny must be a bust."

Although he could remember Tenth Avenue, Tucker had always avoided Times Square. That is, when he could: when the sanitation workers hadn't chased him in that direction. There was too much hustling and bustling there, too much pushing and shoving—and no niceness at all.

There were people dashing everywhere, and bumping each other, and not caring a bit. They all were trying desperately to escape the drizzle, which had now turned to rain.

"I know there's a grille in the street here—that leads down to the subway—" said Harry.

"The subway—" wailed Tucker.

"You'd rather get soaked in the rain? And maybe bonked by a portable radio?"

"The subway," said Tucker, utterly defeated. "And how, might I ask, do you know about the subway?"

"When I was a kitten—"

"Mmm! A lion already!"

"—I did some prowling late at night—and I'm *sure* that there's a grate near here." Harry's eyes flashed left, right —everywhere.

"And what is so safe"—Tucker Mouse was shivering —"about the subway?"

"It's *dry*, and it's *warm*. Now *will you hush up?*"

"Two very good reasons." Tucker wiggled his growing whiskers.

"There it is!" shouted Harry. "Over there! Across the street. That grille in the sidewalk."

"What eyes you have!"

"Come on. But wait for the light—"

In the very small time it takes for a traffic light to change, a mouse and a cat had dashed across Forty-second Street and vanished through a grille in the concrete.

They were just small enough to fit. And then they were gone . . .

Gone underground—to the strange, but lively, warren of the Times Square subway station.

"Isn't it wonderful!" said Harry, awe-struck. He gazed at the stores—for some of the subway stations in New York have stores in them—and at the lunch counters and newspaper stands. But "Oh, those neon lights!"—red, green, blue, a rainbow of colors—they were what fascinated him most.

"I'm scared," said Tucker, who wasn't quite so

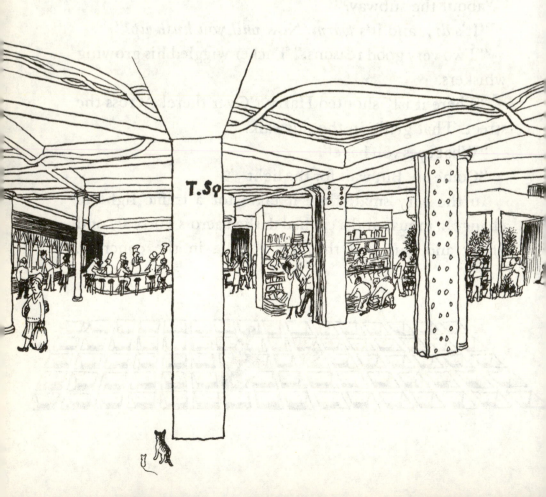

fascinated. "I've never been in a place like this before."

"It's *marvelous!*"

"Sure, marvelous. So where do we live?"

"That remains to be seen. Discovered, I mean. I know the way in, but—"

"*But?*"

"—I don't know the layout. Let's explore."

"I've heard *that* before!" said Tucker Mouse.

But exploring they went, late at night, after hiding behind a trash can which most of the humans didn't bother to use—and when most of the commuters had pushed and crammed their way into the subway cars, to get home.

The station was more quiet then: they could do a little prowling in safety.

Harry was still bewitched by the place, and Tucker had begun to be a little bit bewitched himself—especially by the smells that came from the lunch counters. They made his mouth water.

"I might be happy here, Harry, after all," the mouse admitted breezily.

"So might we both," said Harry. "But we've got to find a place of our own. A private place."

"Like a home, you mean?"

"Exactly. A home."

It got late. And then later. The people riding the subway grew fewer and fewer. Theatergoers, mostly, yawning their long way home.

And still no special place for a kitten and a mouse.

"Let's go over near the Shuttle," said Harry.

"What's that?"

"I think it's just a little short train that goes from Times Square to some place near."

Beside the Shuttle tracks there was a kind of run-down newsstand, all boarded up for the night. But it had a friendly look.

"We could get in there," said Tucker. "Take a look at the cracks in those boards."

"Whoever owns it will open up in the morning—then what?"

Tucker sat on his haunches and sighed. "So the Times Square subway station—another no-place to live."

But Harry, whose eyes were sharper than Tucker's, had been glancing through the gloom. He thought he saw—was it?—yes, it was!—a black opening in the wall.

"There's a hole over there."

"Big deal! A hole."

"Come on—let's look."

The hole was big. And filthy.

"*Yeck!* What a mess," said Tucker.

"It could be cleaned. And also—I don't think too many people know about this hole. It's a very neglected hole."

"And it smells. It's moldy, Harry—"

"*Shhh—*"

"Why shhh? There's nobody here. And no one would want to be."

"I said *'shh!'* " Harry ordered.

Then Tucker heard it, too. There was a faint splashing, somewhere in back.

"A leak, too—"

"Shhh!"

Harry crept to the back of the hole. And even in the dim light that filtered in from the subway, he could see that a trickle of water was falling.

"It's *clean!*" he exclaimed. "Come take a bath!"

"I don't want a bath."

"You need a bath. And this water—it must be a leak from a copper pipe. Clean water, in a subway hole—a true miracle. Now, come on in here, and we'll get clean, too."

Tucker sputtered, and Harry laughed, and in a few minutes, after all their wandering through New York, the dirt they'd collected—inevitable, for vagabonds—had all been washed away.

They let the drifting air dry them off. And the air wasn't dirty, either. It filtered in, very softly, through the opening of the hole.

Many minutes went by.

Then Harry said, "Tucker Mouse, this is our home." He heaved the biggest sigh that has ever been heard from a growing kitten.

"It'll take a lot of cleaning—"

"Oh, Tucker," Harry said, "we're *here*! At last."

"Well, maybe it'll feel more like home when we spruce it up a little."

"It feels pretty good to me already."

"And also when I get my collection."

Harry's eyes widened. "*What* collection?"

"Oh, I don't have it yet," said Tucker airily. "But I intend to form a collection."

"A collection of what?"

"Why—why—of everything! And I'll start with my penny, the one I left back on Tenth Avenue."

"Do you mean to tell me"—Harry's fur prickled—

"that you're going to go all the way back to Tenth Avenue to retrieve one penny?"

"I am, indeed!" said Tucker. "This is one mouse that knows the value of a cent. And besides, it may have been the luck in that penny that found us this place."

"I'm living with a crazy mouse." Harry shook his head. "If you can get all the way to Tenth Avenue, and then back here again, safely—it won't be luck. It'll be another miracle!"

"So you have your miracle with running clean water, and I'll have mine with pennies." He grinned, as a new thought crossed his mind. "And maybe also nickels and dimes. And many other delightful things. But we have to clean this place out first. No collection of mine shall be housed in a dump!"

"To work, then," said Harry.

"To work," said Tucker.

If they had been men, they'd have rolled up their sleeves. But you can't roll up fur that's growing on you— so they just went to work.

And that work took many days—or rather, many nights. For they found it much safer to work at night, when the subway was almost deserted. They threw out chips and chunks of plaster, little bits of concrete, and also the leftover human trash, like a rotten banana peel, that had somehow found its way into the hole.

"You know," said Harry, when they were resting, exhausted, one night, "I think this was a drainpipe once, that got all stuck up. Do you see those watermarks there?"

"Let's hope that we don't clean it out so well that a flood comes crashing down from the street."

"Oh, we won't," said Harry. "It's stopped up for good. Except for my delightful shower. That comes from a different set of pipes, I'm sure."

"And speaking of delightful things," said Tucker, "tomorrow I go for my penny."

Harry sighed. "All right—if we must."

"Not *we*. *I*."

"Tucker, I will not let you go alone. I may still be a kitten, but I'm almost a cat, and—"

"Harry," said Tucker, mouse-proud, "I, too, am growing up. And this deed I must do alone."

Harry narrowed his eyes and looked at his friend. And what he saw quite silenced him. He looked away. "If you must."

"I must."

The next night, a new moon hung in the sky—hung high above the skyscrapers of New York. It seemed like a little silver grin.

Tucker and Harry came up to the sidewalk. By now they knew many secret ways there. A sweet wind from the west had swept the city clean.

"You're really going to do it?" asked Harry.

"I really am," said Tucker. "So long. Be back in a flash!"

59

And the mouse was gone. Harry strained to get a last glimpse of him. Nothing.

The kitten, who *felt* like a kitten now, alone and lonely, went into their home. "Their" home? he wondered. Or was it only his. His alone. He curled and uncurled a dozen times. But sleep would not come.

Late travelers hurried by. And they, too, most of them, looked worried—as if they also had problems that might not be resolved.

Poor human beings—poor animals, thought Harry, sighing.

A young man dropped a token—and then couldn't find it. He said some very nasty words.

But Harry saw where it had landed. He rushed out and pushed the token right next to the young man's feet.

"Hey, wow!" the man shouted. "You are some cat!" He was wearing a fuzzy blue beret. "Thanks, catkins."

But Harry had hurried back to his home.

Where he waited.

And waited . . .

And *waited*! . . . And along with his waiting, his worry grew heavier and heavier.

Until a *plink* sounded in the drainpipe.

"Here's the penny!"

"You *found* it? And got *back*—"

"I think it should be"—Tucker glanced around—"above the mantelpiece!" Just casually he threw in: "I *did* have trouble with that sanitation truck. Those big wheels, you know. Ah, well—I do think the mantelpiece. Except we have no mantelpiece." His eyes wandered here and there. "How about above the entrance to the drainpipe?"

"Great!" Harry looked away and blinked. "Just great. You put it there, though. It's yours."

"It is ours," said Tucker. He placed the penny carefully on a little ledge of stone that stood out above the drainpipe opening. "There. Now, that's a beginning."

And indeed a beginning it was!

For now Tucker Mouse truly knew that collecting things—"scrounging," he called it—was his vocation. (And vocation is what human beings call their life's work.)

He was very lucky, Tucker was, in small change. Apart from pennies, he found a few nickels—and on one glorious afternoon, a quarter.

"The bliss of it," he crooned.

But as well as cash, he also found funny human things. Like a lady's crazy hat: droopy and blue, with a vivid pink feather.

"Will you look at that!"

"I'm looking," said Harry. "It's very ordinary."

"Ordinary is nice," said Tucker Mouse.

And all the time that Tucker Mouse had been collecting—"scrounging"—Harry had been slinking and watching and observing the subway station. And wisely, he observed it all.

He'd observed that there was one man with a red necktie who always made his train if he wore that red necktie. And if he didn't wear it—he lost: the doors closed on his face. His luck is in his necktie, Harry thought. Maybe.

Harry Cat observed a lot. And thought and thought.

"So what are you looking so gloomy for?" asked Tucker one night. He was especially happy that night. He'd found two dimes.

"There are others living here, besides us two," said Harry Cat. "And if you don't believe me, just look across the tracks."

Tucker looked. Six eyes—two by two—were staring at them.

"Who *are* they?"

"*Rats!* And worse than those miserable creatures we met on the docks."

"Rats—"

"And they're big! They live in garbage cans. And they're looking at us."

"Just jealous," said Tucker.

"Maybe," said Harry. "But I want to grow big—very fast. You've been so busy collecting, you haven't seen the eyes. Just look at them!"

Across the subway tracks, those eyes of three rats—steely-greedy—all stared at Tucker and Harry.

"And garbage cans! Who would live there—?"

"Someone hungry"—Tucker tried to make the best of it—"who has no place else to live. You and I weren't doing so well ourselves for a while."

"We never stooped to garbage cans."

Harry grumbled in his throat. "I just don't like the look of those *eyes*. I like the man with the red necktie, and I like the lady who only wears sneakers, but I don't like those eyes. They've been staring at us for *days* now."

"They have?"

"I'll say! And those guys are big, too!"

"Well, you keep an eye on those eyes," said Tucker. "I'm sure it'll be all right."

"Mmm—I wonder," said Harry.

And secretly, although he put on a brave face, Tucker, too, began to worry. He had grown so fond of his collection: the buttons and bits of ribbon, not to mention the money. The thought of anyone preying on them made his fur bristle.

In the course of the next few days, Tucker's worry grew and grew.

He finally had to talk about it. "Harry," he said one

65

night, "you don't think those rats would—would *steal* anything from my collection—"

"They might."

"But *why?* I only collect the things I like. And even the money. I just like to look at those lovely dimes."

"And sometimes roll around in them."

"So who is harmed if every now and then I take a nickel rinse. But rats don't like beautiful things. What *good* would they be to them, anyway."

"I'll give you an example," said Harry. "You remember what you found yesterday?"

Tucker sighed. "Just costume jewelry—but gorgeous!"

"Yes. Well, a rat could steal that pin and drop it in one of the lunch counters. And while the waitresses were fighting over who found it first, he could eat up a pound of hamburger."

"Oh, dear!" Tucker wrung his front paws. "They would *use* my treasures—"

"You bet they would. Because rats *are* users. And they have no sense of beauty at all."

Now Tucker's worry turned to panic. He was so panic-stricken that he almost stopped collecting completely. But not if an especially choice item—like a lady's hairpin —just happened to fall outside the drainpipe opening.

The days wore on . . .

The six eyes stared . . .

And Tucker Mouse thought he just might lose his mouse mind.

66

But even he had to sleep sometimes. He woke up one night—it was very late—and saw Harry staring out into the subway. "Is something wrong?" He jumped to his feet.

"I thought I heard something."

Tucker Mouse did not have time to ask what.

The raid was upon them . . .

However, it didn't feel like a raid at first.

"Hi, guys!" said the biggest rat. "I t'ought we'z oughta get acquainted."

"Oh, delighted to," said Harry Cat, and flashed a warning glance at Tucker.

The strangest thing about these rats was, they all looked alike. One was huge, and one was middle-sized, and one might be called little—although he was at least twice as big as Tucker Mouse. Their fur was a kind of dirty gray—and there *was* dirt on it—but their eyes—oh, their eyes!—were identical: sharp, fierce, piercing, and full of malice.

"I'm Chollie," said the biggest rat.

"I assume that means Charlie," said Harry Cat.

"Yeah, Chollie means Chollie," said Chollie Rat. "An' dis is Spud"—he pointed a claw at the middle-sized rat—"so called cuz potatoes is his favorite food. An' da runt is the Bump. Fa da reason dat looms at da end of his nose."

The Bump had a nervous laugh—if one could call it a laugh. It was more like a high, queer shriek. "Yeah, the Bump. I'm the Bump." He squealed with delight.

"I wish you wouldn't do that," said Tucker. "It's very upsetting."

"So, upset," said the Bump. "We all got our problems." His mad laughter fluttered insanely, again.

"I am not happy, Harry," Tucker said to his friend.

"Why?" said Chollie. "It's just a frien'ly call."

"Yeah, so's us guys can get to know youse guys," said Spud.

Tucker shot Harry a very nervous look. "In fact, I am very *un*happy, Harry."

"You notice how nice da little mouse smells?" said Chollie to Spud.

"I took a shower before retiring tonight," said Tucker. "It's a practice I strongly urge all you three to adopt."

This remark brought forth the wildest giggling yet from the Bump.

By now, inch by inch, the rats had edged their way into the drainpipe. Tucker and Harry found themselves backed against one wall.

"So—a mouse an' a kitten livin' togetha," said Chollie. "A very strange combination."

"I am *not* a kitten," said Harry, with as much conviction as he could. "I'm a *cat*."

"Youse still are a kitten—with a kitten's little whiskers." Chollie flicked Harry's whiskers with one claw. Then he flicked his own. "Whereas dese are da whiskas of a full-grown rat!"

"Well, it's been nice to meet you," squeaked Tucker. "If there's ever anything you should need—like a shower—"

"Need—" said Chollie, and a glint of teeth appeared behind an evil smile. "We don't *need* nothin'. But there's somethin' we *want*." The sound that came from his mouth was part snarl, part growl, and part hiss. "We want what we been seein' you rake in dis hole, my little freaky-furry friend. An' we're gonna get it! So don't fight

70

—don't argue—just hand over all you got!"

"My Life Savings—" shrieked Tucker.

"If dat's what you call da loot—yeah! Ya life's savin's."

"I will not!" And shivering though he was—a bit from the dampness still in his fur, since he hadn't dried himself too well earlier—Tucker Mouse stamped his foot. "No! Never!"

"Yeah, ya will," said Chollie, in a quiet, deadly kind of voice—as if bored, as if the whole awful transaction had already been completed. "Or else I'll hoit ya very bad. An' den take da stuff anyway."

At that, Harry Cat blew up. "I told you," he shouted at Tucker. "These are *bums*. They'd plant a dime just to bite someone's leg who was picking it up."

"Not a bad idea," chuckled Chollie Rat. "Da kitty's got a sense of humor. An' by da way, we'll be back every month to collect what youse have picked up in da meantime."

"No—" Now Harry, too, spoke quietly, although his voice broke a little, since Chollie was right: he wasn't a cat yet. "No, you will not. You will not take one item of my friend's possessions. And furthermore, you will leave these premises which are our home—right now!—and go back to whichever filthy garbage can you call *your* home."

For a moment Chollie Rat just stared at this dopey little kitten, whose fur was still fuzzy, and who had challenged him, given *him*, Chollie Rat, an order to go.

But for only a moment did Chollie Rat stare.

Then he lunged at Harry and sank his hideous sharp teeth in the kitten's shoulder. Harry screamed—as a cat can scream, not simply yowl—for the pain was horrible.

But Tucker didn't scream—he roared! A real roar for a very small mouse. Then he went for Chollie, and bit his tail.

"Ow! *Ow!*" And the rat let go of Harry. Tucker bit in deeper.

Chollie bared all his teeth. And Tucker knew that, for him at least, the fight was over. He might as well be dead.

But he wasn't dead. Because, once those fangs were out of his shoulder, Harry jumped on Chollie's back and started clawing, as best he could with claws that weren't yet grown.

Meanwhile, the two other rats had been gawking. They couldn't believe that a kitten and a mouse would fight back—and particularly at their boss, Chollie Rat. But now they knew they had to join the battle, too. They had to help Chollie, because if they didn't, he'd skin them alive.

A frenzy—a frantic and furious chaos—of claws, paws, teeth, tails, now occurred. No one was winning.

But suddenly Chollie Rat shouted, *"Hold it!"*

In the fury—the fighting—the scratching and biting—the whole situation had ended like this: Harry Kitten, who now was definitely Harry Cat, had managed to flatten Chollie. The rat lay on his back, and Harry sprawled over him. And Tucker Mouse, with the tiny instinct that small persecuted people have, had raised one small but very sharp claw above Chollie's tender nose.

"Stop! Stop!" shouted Chollie. "Oo! Oo! My nose—"

"You better stop," Tucker said. For a mouse he suddenly felt very strong. "And you'd better tell your friends to go home. Otherwise—" It was horrible—but—to save their home— "Otherwise, I'm going to claw a good gouge from your nose." And he only hoped that his claws were big enough to carry out his threat.

"Go on, you guys!" whimpered Chollie Rat. He didn't sound one single bit like his former bragging and blustering self. "Go on! Back to da gahbitch can. My nose—! Ooo—"

"Oh, wow!" said the Bump, who hadn't said a single
word till then. "An' I t'ought *I* was da cowahd." He
tittered again.

The Bump and Spud backed out of the drainpipe.

Very gingerly, Harry and Tucker let Chollie go. And
he went *fast*!—out of shame as well as pain.

Neither mouse nor cat had the strength to speak. For at least five minutes there was only relief—peace.

"He said they'd be back in a month," Tucker Mouse finally found the breath to say.

"Now, don't worry!" Harry Cat had long since realized that the best way, the only way, to quiet his friend was to flatten him gently on the floor with a paw, claws in. "With all the lunch stands here, I'll be able to eat a lot. And in one month"—he reared up on his hind legs and showed off his growing muscles—"in just one month, I'll be so big that all the rats in New York will tremble. Most of all, those hooligans!"

"Very impressive, I must say," said Tucker, who knew

that for the rest of his life he would always be a mouse.

"And by the way"—Harry tapped Tucker's head—"Mousiekins, you saved my life. By biting that nasty creature's tail."

"Yes, and you saved my Life Savings," said Tucker.

Harry Cat had to laugh at that. And it wasn't just the purring murmur of a cat's delight. It was more like the howling yowling of mirth. And happiness. And safety. And home. "And of course they are equally important. My life—and your life savings, that is."

"Oh, Harry, I didn't mean—"

But Tucker was abruptly distracted. A splash of silver fell at his feet.

"Come on, Master Mouse! I was only kidding—"

"Look, Harry."

At a certain hour of the night a ray of moonlight, if the moon was full, fell through a grating, above, in Times Square. And fell like a silent poem—a prayer—in front of the drainpipe where Harry and Tucker now lived.

They both looked at the silvery light. And then they went out, to get the feel of it on their backs.

The moonlight made the fur of both animals shine. It felt as if it were shining inside them, too.

Tucker Mouse was silent. And then he coughed. The late stillness of the subway station—so beautiful and difficult—just had to be broken.

And then it was really broken—harshly: a clattering train rushed in.

One man ran to catch it. And made it.

A lady cried, "Oh, please wait!" The man firmly held the door open for her. "Oh, thank you," she said. The train sped away.

"I'm glad she caught it," murmured Tucker. But Harry said nothing. He shone.

FLIP ME OVER

to keep reading about Chester Cricket and his friends!

FLIP ME OVER
to keep reading about Chester Cricket's friends!

"How *can* I ever thank you?" said Chester.

"Don't bother, Chester C. Just glad to meet someone who loves New York as much as I do. And come on over to Bryant Park again. I'll be there—one branch or another. Night, Cricket."

"Night, Lulu."

She fluttered away.

Chester bounded through the grate and hopped as fast as he could toward the drainpipe. He hoped that Tucker and Harry were back. Tonight he *really* had an adventure to tell them!

And all the while, the dream city drew nearer. It seemed to Chester like some huge spiderweb. The streets were the strands, all hung with multicolored lights. "Oh, Lulu, it's—I don't know—it's—"

"Hush!" said the pigeon. "Just look and enjoy." They were flying amid the buildings now. "Enjoy, and remember."

Chester Cricket could not contain himself. He gave a chirp—not a song, just one chirp—but that single chirp said, 'I love this! *I love it!*'

Then there was Times Square, erupting with colors. Chester pointed out the grating he'd come through—and Lulu landed next to it.

on an even keel. But once or twice, just for the fun of it, she tilted her wings without warning. They zoomed up, fast—then dipped down, faster—a roller coaster in the empty air.

"You wait till I fly you back," said the pigeon. "You'll see how that dream can turn real."

The wind, which had been a hindrance before, was a help now. Lulu coasted almost all the way back to Manhattan, only lifting a wing now and then to keep them

with tiny lights on their cables—that joined the island to the lands all round.

"Oh, wow! We're in luck!" exclaimed Lulu. With a flick of her wing, she gestured down. Almost right below them, it seemed, an ocean liner was gliding by, its rigging, like the bridges, strung with hundreds of silver bulbs.

An airplane passed over them. And even *it* had lights on its wings!

Through his eyes, Chester's heart became flooded with wonder. "It's like—it's like a dream of a city, at night."

"Now, just look around!" said Lulu proudly, as if all
of New York belonged to her. "And don't anybody ever
tell *this* pigeon that there's a more beautiful sight in the
world."

Chester did as he was told. He first peered behind.
There was Staten Island. And off to the left, New Jersey.
To the right, quite a long way away, was Brooklyn. And
back across the black water, with a dome of light glowing
over it, the heart of the city—Manhattan.

And bridges! Bridges everywhere—all pricked out

At last, Chester saw where the pigeon was heading. On a little island, off to the right, Chester made out the form of a very big lady. Her right hand was holding something up. Of course it was the Statue of Liberty, but Chester had no way of knowing that. In the Old Meadow in Connecticut he never had gone to school—at least not to a school where the pupils use books. His teacher back there had been Nature herself.

Lulu landed at the base of the statue, puffing and panting to get back her breath. She told him a little bit about the lady—a gift from the country of France, it was, and very precious to America—but she hadn't flown him all that way just to give him a history lesson.

"Hop on again, Chester C.!" she commanded—and up they flew to the torch that the lady was holding. Lulu found a perch on the north side of it, so the wind from the south wouldn't bother them.

the wind was against them too, which made the flying more difficult. Chester held his peace, and watched the city slip beneath them.

They reached the Battery, which is that part of lower New York where a cluster of skyscrapers rise up like a grove of steel trees. But Lulu didn't stop there.

With a gasp and an even tighter hold on her feathers, Chester realized that they'd flown right over the end of Manhattan. There was dark churning water below them. And this was no tame little lake, like the one in Central Park. It was the great deep wide bay that made New York such a mighty harbor. But Lulu showed no sign whatsoever of slowing. Her wings, like beautiful trustworthy machines, pumped on and on and on and on.

"Grab on!" a familiar voice shouted. "Tight! Tighter! That's it."

Chester gladly did as he was told.

"*Whooooey!*" Lulu breathed a sigh of relief. "Thought I'd never find you. Been around this darn building at least ten times."

Chester wanted to say, 'Thank you, Lulu,' but he was so thankful he couldn't get one word out till they'd reached a level where the air was friendly and gently buoyed them up.

But before he could even open his mouth, the pigeon —all ready for another adventure—asked eagerly, "Where now, Chester C.?"

"I guess I better go back to the drainpipe, Lulu. I'm kind of tired."

"Aw, no—!" complained Lulu, who'd been having fun.

"You know, I'm really not all that used to getting blown off the Empire State Building—"

"Oh, all right," said the pigeon. "But first there's one thing you *gotta* see!"

Flying just below the level of turbulent air—good pilot that she was—Lulu headed south, with Chester clinging to the back of her neck. He felt much safer up there, and her wings didn't block out as much of the view as they'd thought. He wanted to ask where they were going, but he sensed from the strength and regularity of her wingbeats that it was to be a rather long flight. And

Lulu *almost* fell off—but Chester *did!* In an instant his legs and feelers were torn away from the pigeon's leg, and before he could say, 'Old Meadow, farewell!' he was tumbling down through the air. One moment the city appeared above him—that meant that he was upside down; then under him—he was right side up; then everything slid from side to side.

He worked his wings, tried to hold them stiff to steady himself—no use, no use! The gleeful wind was playing with him. It was rolling him, throwing him back and forth, up and down, as a cork is tossed in the surf of a storm. And minute by minute, when he faced that way, the cricket caught glimpses of the floors of the Empire State Building plunging upward as he plunged down.

Despite his panic, his mind took a wink of time off to think: 'Well, *this* is something that can't have happened to many crickets before!' (He was right, too—it hadn't. And just at that moment Chester wished that it wasn't happening to *him*.)

He guessed, when New York was in the right place again, that he was almost halfway down. The people were looking more and more like people—he heard the cars' engines—and the street and the sidewalk looked *awfully* hard! Then—

Whump! He landed on something both hard and soft. It was hard inside, all muscles and bones, but soft on the surface—feathers!

second—worse yet—a sudden gust of wind sprang up, as
if a hand gave them both a push. Lulu almost fell off the
Empire State.

And they made it! Lulu gripped the pinnacle of the TV antenna with both her claws, accidentally pinching one of Chester's legs as she did so. The whole of New York glowed and sparkled below them.

Now it is strange, but it is true, that although there are many mountains higher than even the tallest buildings, and airplanes can fly much higher than mountains, *nothing* ever seems quite so high as a big building that's been built by men. It suggests our own height to ourselves, I guess.

Chester felt as if not only a city but the entire world was down there where he could look at it. He almost couldn't see the people. 'My gosh!' he thought. 'They look just like bugs.' And he had to laugh at that: like bugs—perhaps crickets—moving up and down the sidewalks. And the cars, the buses, the yellow taxis, all jittered along like miniatures. He felt that kind of spinning sensation inside his head that had made him dizzy on the way up. But he refused to close his eyes. It was too much of an adventure for that.

"Lulu, my foot," said Chester, "you're stepping on it. Could you please—"

"Ooo, I'm sorry," the pigeon apologized. She lifted her claw.

And just at that moment two bad things happened. The first was, Chester caught sight of an airplane swooping low to land at LaGuardia Airport across the East River. The dip of it made his dizziness worse. And the

ward, around the building, floor past floor, and ap-
proached their final destination: the television antenna
tower on the very top.

But even the loveliest intervals end.

Song done—one moment more of silent delight—and then Lulu said, "Come on, Chester C., let me show you some more of my town"—by which she meant New York.

"Okay," said Chester, and climbed on her claw again.

"I want you to see it *all* now!" said Lulu. Her wings were beating strongly, rhythmically. "And the best place for that is the Empire State Building."

They rose higher and higher. And the higher they went, the more scared Chester got. Flying up Fifth Avenue had been fun as well as frightening, but now they were heading straight for the top of one of the tallest buildings in all the world.

Chester looked down—the world swirled beneath him —and felt as if his stomach turned over. Or maybe his brain turned around. But something in him felt queasy and dizzy. "Lulu—" he began anxiously, "—I think—"

"Just hold on tight!" Lulu shouted down. "And trust in your feathered friend!"

What Chester had meant to say was that he was afraid he was suffering from a touch of acrophobia—fear of heights. (And perched on a pigeon's claw, on your way to the top of the Empire State, is not the best place to find that you are afraid of great heights.) But even if Lulu hadn't interrupted, the cricket couldn't have finished his sentence. His words were forced back into his throat. For the wind, which had been just a breeze beside the lake, was turning into a raging gale as they spiraled up-

only sycamore trees in the park. The cricket could smell birches, beeches, and maples—elms, oaks—almost as many kinds of trees as Connecticut itself had to offer. And there was the moon!—the crescent moon—reflected in a little lake. Sounds, too, rose up to him: the shooshing of leaves, the nighttime countryside whispering of insects and little animals, and—best of all—a brook that was arguing with itself, as it splashed over rocks. The miracle of Central Park, a sheltered wilderness in the midst of the city, pierced Chester Cricket's heart with joy.

"Oh, can we go down?" he shouted up. "Lulu?—please!"

" 'Course, Chester C." The pigeon slowed and tilted her wings. "Anything you want. But let's not call on my relatives. They're a drag, and they're all asleep by now anyway."

"I don't want to *visit* anybody!" said Chester, as Lulu Pigeon coasted down through the air, as swiftly and neatly and accurately as a little boy's paper airplane, and landed beside the lake. "All I want is—is—" He didn't know how to say it exactly, but all Chester wanted was to sit beside that shimmering lake—a breeze ruffled its surface—and look at the jiggling reflection of the moon, and enjoy the sweet moisture and the tree-smelling night all around him.

And chirp. Above all, Chester wanted to chirp. Which he did, to his heart's content. And to Lulu Pigeon's heart's content, too.

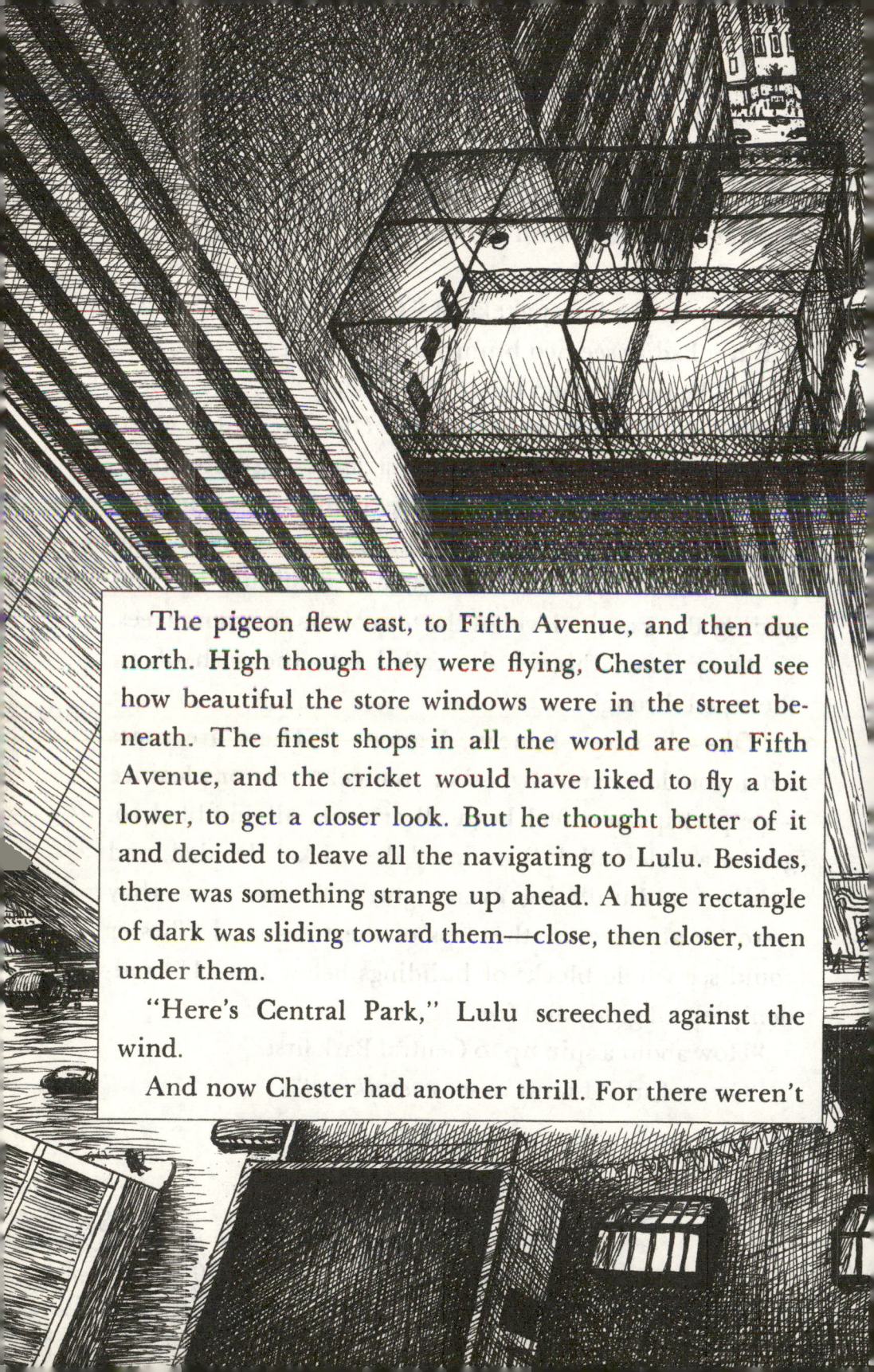

The pigeon flew east, to Fifth Avenue, and then due north. High though they were flying, Chester could see how beautiful the store windows were in the street beneath. The finest shops in all the world are on Fifth Avenue, and the cricket would have liked to fly a bit lower, to get a closer look. But he thought better of it and decided to leave all the navigating to Lulu. Besides, there was something strange up ahead. A huge rectangle of dark was sliding toward them—close, then closer, then under them.

"Here's Central Park," Lulu screeched against the wind.

And now Chester had another thrill. For there weren't

"First I gotta rev up."

Lulu flapped her wings a few times. And then—before Chester could gasp with delight—*they were flying!*

To fly!—oh, be flying!

"Sorry for the bumpy takeoff," said Lulu.

But it hadn't seemed bumpy to Chester at all.

"It'll be better when I gain altitooode."

Back in Connecticut, in the Old Meadow, when Chester made one of his mightiest leaps—usually showing off in front of a friend like Joe Skunk—he sometimes reached as high as six feet. But in seconds Lulu had passed that height, and in less than a minute she was gliding along at the level of the tops of the sycamore trees.

"Okay down there?" she called into the rush of air they sped through.

"Oh—oh, sure—I mean, I guess—" There are times when you don't know whether you feel terror or pleasure —or perhaps you feel both all at once, all jumbled together wonderfully! "I'm fine!" the cricket decided, and held on to Lulu's leg even tighter. Because now they were far above even the tops of the trees, and Chester could see whole blocks of buildings below him. He suddenly felt all giddy and free.

"How about a spin up to Central Park first?"

"Great, Lulu! I want to see *everything!*"

she gave a big scratch and exclaimed, "I got it! You sit on my claw—take the left one there—and wrap a couple of feelers around." Chester hesitated a minute or two. He was quite sure no cricket had ever done *this* before.

"Go on! Get on!" Lulu ordered. "You're in for a thrill."

"All right—" Chester mounted the pigeon's claw, with a feeling that was partly excitement, part fear, and held on tight.

fly with the times. That's why I moved down here tooo Bryant Park. It's nearer where the action is. Yooo get what I mean?"

"I guess so," said Chester—although he didn't understand her completely. Lulu had a strange New York way of talking that was sort of hard to understand. But Chester meant to try, because he was beginning to like this pigeon very much. Even if there might be some kookoo bird in her.

"But don't you *ever* see any of your family now?" he asked.

"Oh, shooor." Lulu scratched the earth with one claw. "Every once in a while I fly up to Central Park. There's an elm tree up there reserved solely for the Stuyvesant Pigeon clan, if yooo please!"

"Where's Central Park?" asked the cricket.

"You don't know where Central *Park* is?" said Lulu. "Big beautiful Central Park!—the best place in the city—"

"I guess I don't," Chester apologized. He explained that Mario had taken him on several excursions, but not, as yet, to Central Park.

"Say!" exclaimed Lulu. "How would you like a real tooor of Nooo York? One that only a pigeon could give."

"Well, I'd love one," said Chester, "but—"

"Hop on my back, just behind my neck. Nope—" Lulu bobbed her head jerkily, trying to think. "—Yooo couldn't see down through my wings too well." Then

New Amsterdam 1650

"Now, what about *you?*" he asked, when he'd finished his own strange tale.

"Oh, me!" Lulu chortled delightfully. "I'm what yooo'd call a pecuoooliar pigeon. Or maybe even a koo-koo bird."

Then Lulu told Chester *her* story. It seems that she came from a very old and aristocratic family of pigeons. In fact, her great-great-great—she couldn't remember how many greats—grandmother and grandfather, the Hynrik Stuyvesant Pigeons, claimed to have crossed the Atlantic clinging to one of the yardarms of a vessel sailing to New Amsterdam. Lulu explained that that was what New York was called when it was still a Dutch city, before the English took over.

"They claimed they were 'bored' with the Old World and wanted tooo explore the New Frontiers," Lulu squawked derisively. "But I just think they couldn't make a living in Holland any more."

Anyway, the Hynrik Stuyvesant Pigeons and all their descendants prospered greatly in the great New World. They became probably the most famous and respected pigeon family on the island of Manhattan—so famous and respected, indeed, that now they refused to eat any bread crumbs except those that were thrown out on Park Avenue.

"But about a year ago," said Lulu, "I had a beakful of all that ritzy jazz, so I told my snooooty relatives bye-bye and just flapped out. I decided that I'd rather, like,

Chester told Lulu all about himself: being trapped in the picnic basket, and then found by Mario in the subway station, and then being "adopted," as you might say, by Tucker Mouse and Harry Cat.

"Dooo all the crickets in Connecticut sound like that?" asked Lulu, bobbing her head in disbelief.

"Oh, I don't know," answered Chester bashfully. As a matter of fact, he'd been told by a well-traveled robin named John that he was the finest musician in the state, but that wasn't the kind of thing you would tell a complete stranger.

get one thing straight. You're not going to eat me, are you?"

"Ooooo, goodness no!" and Lulu Pigeon laughed. "I only eat bread crumbs. There's the cuoootest little old lady who lives at the corner of 101st Street and West End Avenue. She has a shelf outside her bedroom window, and every morning it's loaded with bread crumbs—all for *me!*"

"That's very nice," said Chester Cricket. "Now"—he was always a little embarrassed—"would you really like to hear another song?"

"I would love tooo!" enthused Lulu Pigeon. "Go, Cricket, go!"

With considerable relief, Chester chirped her one of his favorite songs.

"Man, that is the *greatest!*" Lulu exclaimed. "Now what is your *story*, Chester C.? How come you're singing down here in the city instead of out in the sticks somewhere?"

said a burbly voice behind him. "What A plump country cricket, I dooo believe." was so surprised—no, shocked—that he leaped air and whirled around. And there, standing in k of him, was the biggest pigeon he'd ever seen. It had a strange gleam in its eye.

Now, back in the Old Meadow, Chester had known several rather large birds. Beatrice Pheasant and he got along very well. But there was also Lou Blue Jay and Andy Blackbird, and Chester avoided them as much as he could. Because most of the big birds that he knew had one very special favorite meal: a nice plump savory country cricket.

"Um—er—" Chester stuttered. He didn't quite know what a person said when he might be gobbled up in a minute.

"That was beoootiful!" cooed the pigeon.

"You *liked* my song—?" Chester gasped, amazed.

"Grooovy!" the pigeon crooned.

'Well, for heaven's sake!' Chester thought to himself. 'I suppose I shouldn't be too surprised. If a cat and a mouse can live in a drainpipe, maybe me and a pigeon can also be friends.'

"I'm awfully glad!" he said out loud.

"More! More!" demanded the pigeon. "By the way, name's Lulu—" She pronounced it 'Looolooo.' "What's yours?"

"Chester Cricket," said Chester. "But—um—er—let's

down into it. For two wee[...]
concrete, on asphalt, and s[...]
had made his legs quite so[...]
the lovely springy soil itself.[...]

The sycamore tree rose st[...]
see the moon again, riding th[...]
tered down and landed beside[...]
out of it. And was it delicious[...]
and chocolate candies were all[...] was
nothing like a simple leaf to sui[...]cket's appetite.

Out of sheer pleasure in feeling the earth, and eating
a leaf, and sitting outside in the night, Chester had to
begin to chirp. The notes came softly at first, and slowly,
as if the cricket were testing the sound; but then more
and more clearly they rang through the park. Chester
was perfectly content when he sang. He could hear the
chirping and feel his wings rubbing together, but he
thought of nothing. A happy stillness filled his heart. Sai
Fong, the Chinese gentleman who had sold Mario the
cricket cage, had said that a cricket always sings the song
of truth—the song of a person who knows all things.
That may be so, but for Chester his song was simply the
music of his delight at being alive.

The song went on for several minutes. It was slow,
then fast; then low, and then high. Like a thread of
bright silk, it ran through the darkness. And then it
ended. Chester never knew why a song ended. He could
feel the end coming—and the music was over.

excited—and also so small—that no one saw him. And perhaps even the police wouldn't have minded if they'd known how eager he was to get to those trees.

The park was raised six steps above sidewalk level. Chester took them two at a time, and his last jump landed him—plop!—on real earth. It felt so good to dig his feet

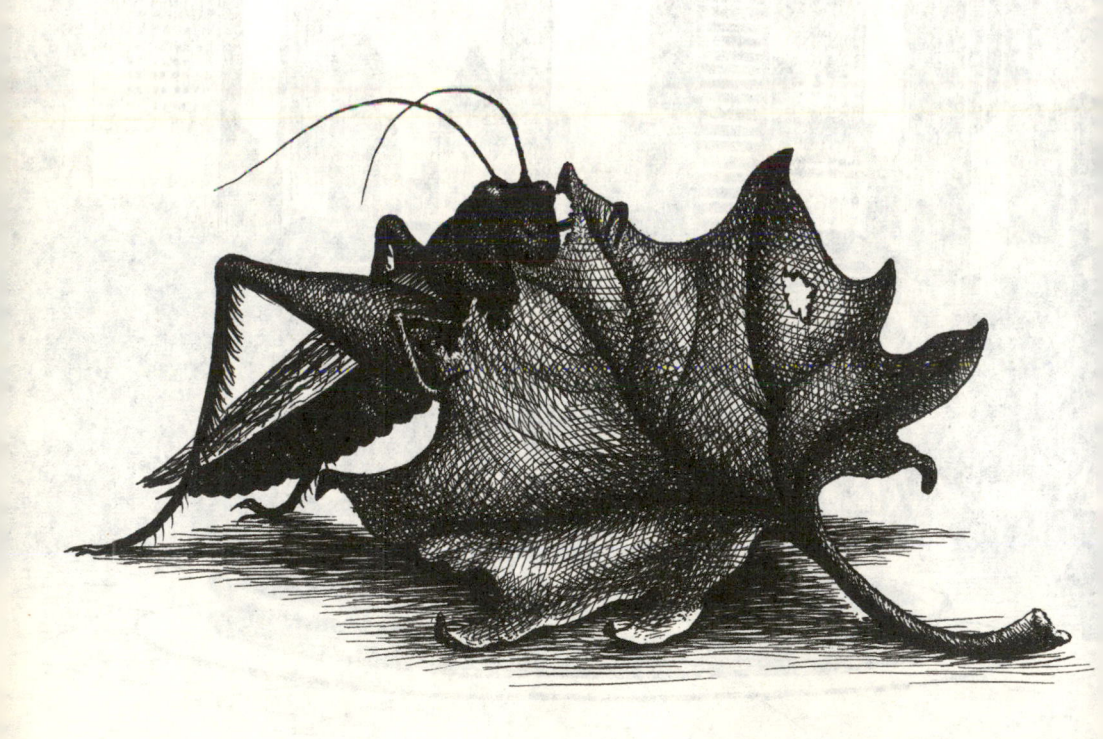

Chester began jumping down Forty-second Street, following the smell of the sycamore tree. He had to make his hops low to keep from hitting the bottom of the cars that were parked beside the curb. Every so often, he would pass by the brightly lit entrance to a movie theater and a gust of cool air from the air conditioning blew over him. His mood of homesickness had changed completely. He was by himself, exploring—adventuring, in fact!—and he'd just crossed Broadway. He felt that if he could cross Broadway—well, he could do anything! Sometimes, just out of high spirits, he stopped and chirped a few times. But nobody heard, through the city's din.

Chester reached the end of the block. There was another street to cross—the Avenue of the Americas—but it wasn't nearly as busy as Broadway. And diagonally across from the curb on which he stood, Chester saw a remarkable thing: trees—and shrubs—and a fountain that dripped water into a marble basin. There was actually a little park, tucked away in the heart of New York City—and only a block from Times Square! He could see the sycamore tree—in fact, there were lots of them, arranged in rows, with cement walks between them. It was surely a sight to gladden a country cricket's heart.

As soon as the light changed, Chester launched right out into the street, ahead of all the human beings. When he got to the other side, he couldn't wait and crossed Forty-second Street against the red light. That is called jaywalking and it is against the law. But Chester was so

But it did. The cricket made three mighty leaps, and the last one landed him on the other side of the street. He crouched in the gutter, against the curb, panting. People were stepping over him onto the sidewalk, but Chester was safe. He hopped under a car and heaved a sigh of relief.

(Of course he couldn't know it, but he was the first cricket to cross Broadway since 1789, when it was still a country lane.)

For a second, Chester couldn't think where he was.
Then everything came back to him, but it was too late
to move. The light had changed back to red. Headlights
were rushing down on him from left and from right.
Chester flattened himself on the street.

He was right in the middle, on the white line. Cars
came whizzing by, in back and in front. One turned the
corner and went completely over him. The wind from
its tires almost tore him loose. But Chester clung to the
white line with all his might. He didn't think that the
light would *ever* change!

"About sixty seconds," he said. Sometimes it helps to talk to yourself, when you're concentrating.

Then he stood up on his hind legs and tried to judge how far it was to the other side of Broadway. "Not more than thirty feet," he decided. "Now let me see. I can do three feet to a jump—so that takes ten jumps. And I *certainly* should be able to make ten jumps in one minute." So, by all his figuring, he ought to make it. But there wasn't going to be much time to spare.

He got on the very edge of the curb and flexed his legs, like a high jumper in the Olympic Games. This was by far the most serious jumping in Chester's whole life—and *much* more dangerous than crossing the brook back home.

The light changed.

He sprang out—a high arc—into the street. One.

He jumped again. Two.

There were human beings all around him, coming and going across Broadway. He had to keep going zigzag to miss them.

His third hop put him in the middle of the street. "May make it in only eight," he said.

But then something dreadful happened. A man who was in a terrible hurry cut into one of Chester's arcs. That's frequently what happens: somebody bumbles into your plans. Once the cricket had left the ground, he couldn't stop, and he hit the man right in the waist. The jolt stunned him and he fell back onto the asphalt. Luckily, there was no one coming behind him.

was down there, though, somewhere—he knew it. And he had to find it! Chester had never struck off on his own in the city before, but he couldn't resist. He felt that he'd be all right again if he could just sit under that sycamore tree for a few blissful minutes.

The best way to go, he decided, would be in the gutter. That way he'd miss the people on the sidewalk and the cars in the street. The worst problem was going to be getting across Broadway. He measured the time the light was green.

There was a soft wind blowing, playing up and down Forty-second Street. Chester leaned against the Times Building, letting it cool him after his long climb up. He could smell all kinds of city smells in the breeze: hamburgers and hot dogs and soda pop, and gasoline from the automobiles, and even the strange, dry odor of concrete buildings. But in among the other smells there was one scent that he couldn't quite place. Yet he knew he had smelled it somewhere before. He took another sniff—and suddenly he jumped up on his six feet. It was a tree! He sniffed again. And a sycamore tree at that—one of his favorites. He hadn't been near a tree for so long he'd forgotten what one smelled like!

The sidewalk wasn't too crowded just then, so he hopped out to the edge of the curb. Squatting down, he collected his strength and then made his highest jump into the air. But he still couldn't see the tree. There was nothing but hundreds of bobbing headlights and human beings rushing back and forth. It

as Tucker's cluttered home, but he hadn't been beyond there since his first night in Times Square, and he lost his way several times. His long antennae were a big help, however. They were perfect for feeling his way along dark drainpipes. It took Chester half an hour of back-tracking and starting again, trying out the different holes, to reach the sidewalk. But finally he found a grate in the pavement—and there he was, right out in the open!

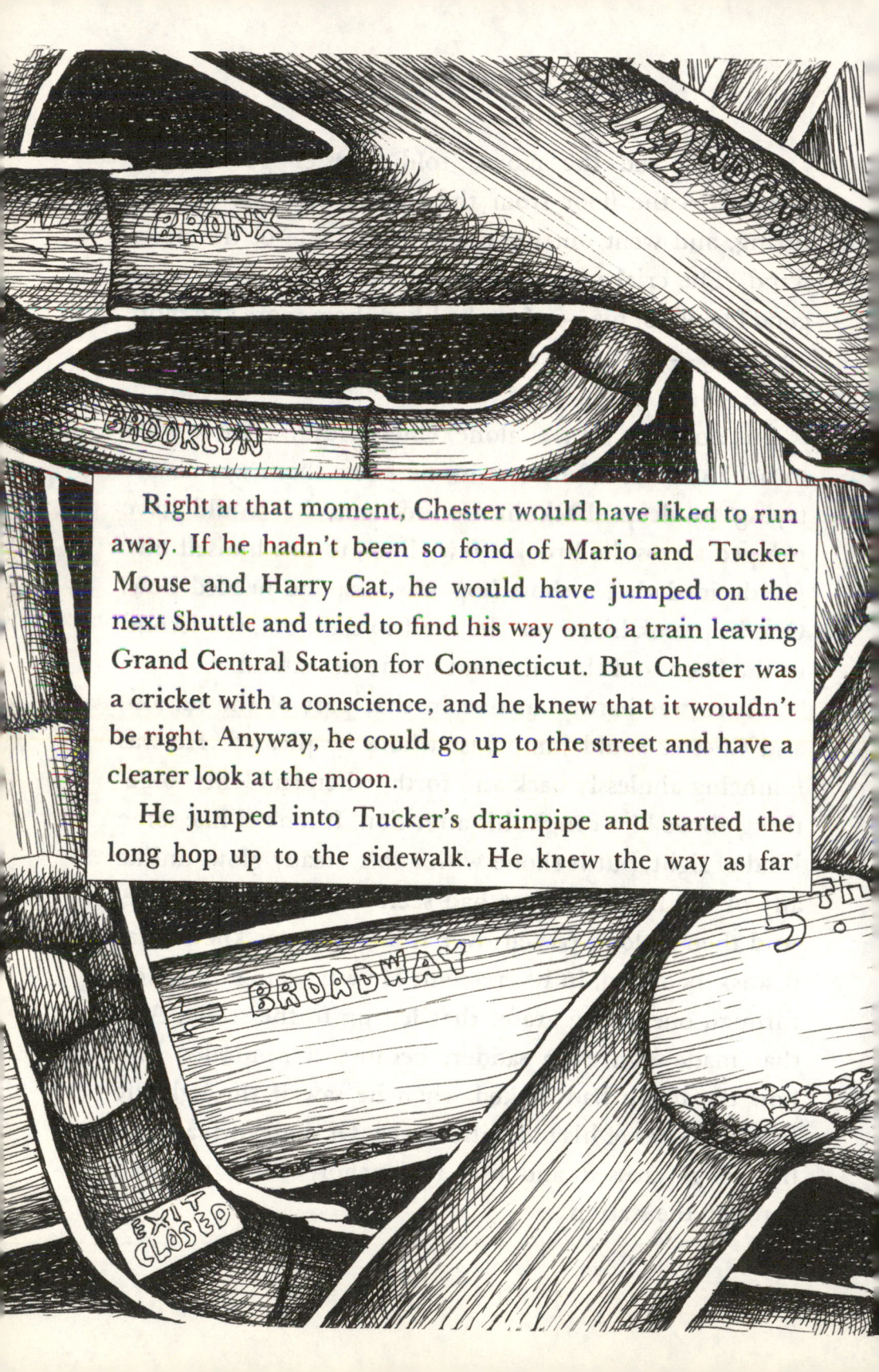

Right at that moment, Chester would have liked to run away. If he hadn't been so fond of Mario and Tucker Mouse and Harry Cat, he would have jumped on the next Shuttle and tried to find his way onto a train leaving Grand Central Station for Connecticut. But Chester was a cricket with a conscience, and he knew that it wouldn't be right. Anyway, he could go up to the street and have a clearer look at the moon.

He jumped into Tucker's drainpipe and started the long hop up to the sidewalk. He knew the way as far

The cat and the mouse told Chester good night, jumped to the floor from the stool where they'd been sitting, and went out the crack in the side of the newsstand. The cricket was grateful they'd gone. They were good friends of his—in fact, he liked them more and more every day—but there came times when a cricket had to be alone.

But now that he *was* alone, Chester didn't know what to do. In the mood he was in, he knew there was no use trying to sleep. Back in Connecticut, he would have jumped across the brook a few times, to tire himself out. He decided that a short hop was what he needed now. One leap took him from the shelf to the stool, the second to the floor, and the third out of the newsstand.

There was hardly anyone in that part of the station, and Chester could jump just where he pleased. He was bouncing aimlessly back and forth, when suddenly something above him caught his attention. It looked like some kind of light, but it shone with a soft, steady glow, unlike any of the lights Chester had seen in New York before. And then a cloud passed over it and Chester knew what it was: the moon, in its crescent. He was seeing the moon through one of the grates that led up to the street. And that made him even sadder, because it reminded him how the moon had looked when he saw it through the thin branches of his old willow tree. Of their own accord, his wings crossed and one melancholy chirp sounded through the station.

"Okay," said Tucker. He might not be a highbrow, but Tucker Mouse knew enough not to pry into other people's problems when they didn't want to talk about them. "Come on, Harry. Let's you and me go. I could stand a little singing and dancing tonight."

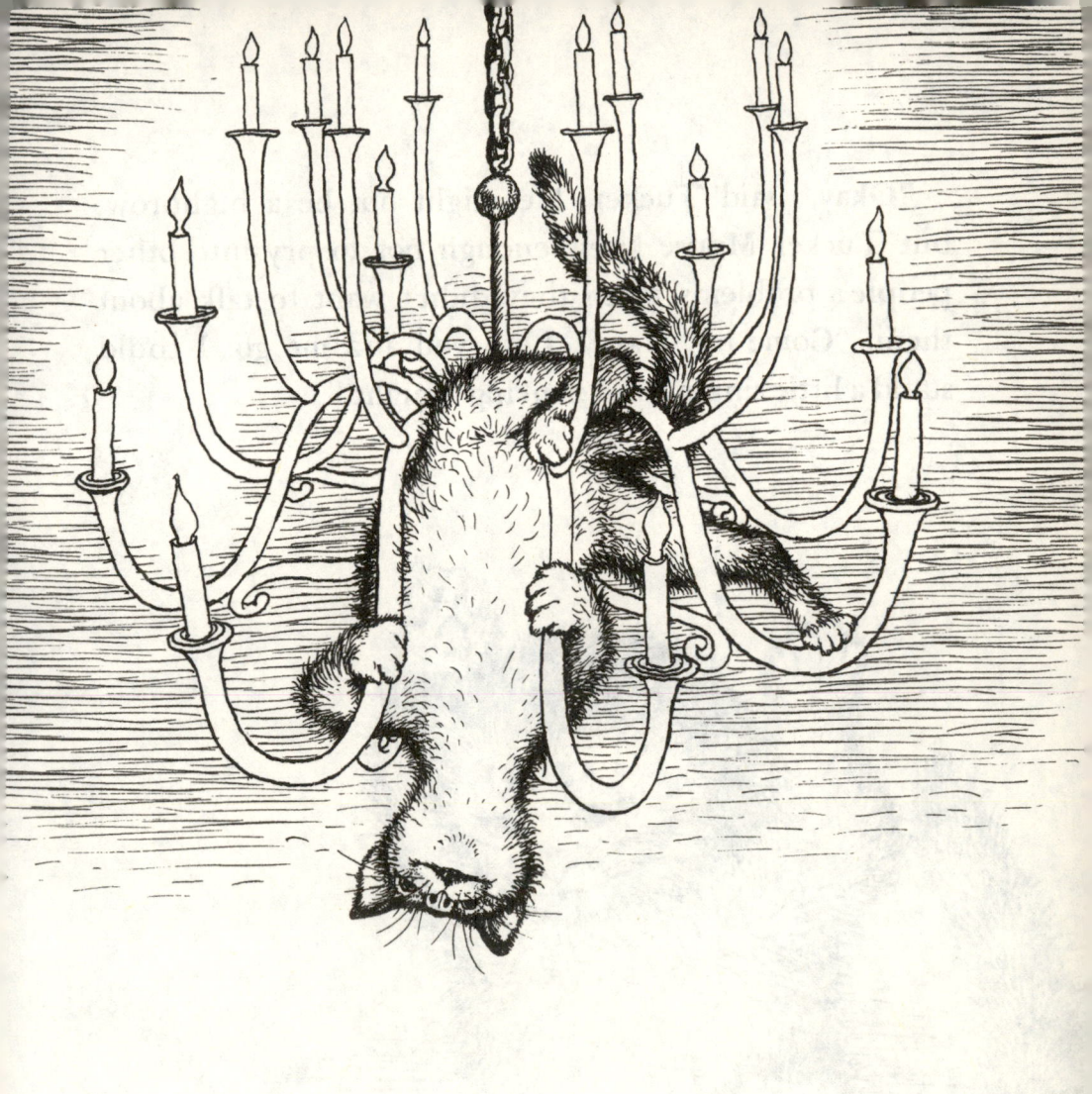

from the way Chester spoke that there was something
bothering him.

"Not really," said the cricket. "But I don't feel like
going out again today."

"Naturally I enjoy the films," Harry Cat said, and flicked his long tail around his forelegs. "But I really prefer the legitimate theater. For the past five years I've been the most eager theatergoer in New York. I've stood in the balcony, I've hidden backstage—why, once I even hung on a chandelier. There's nothing I wouldn't do to see a good play. Ah, the glamour—the romance of the theater! I love it!"

"That's nice," said Chester. "Have you been to many plays, Tucker?" He was still feeling blue, and didn't want to talk much.

"A few," the mouse answered indifferently. "I like musical comedies more."

"What a boor!" said Harry Cat.

"So I'm not a highbrow," said Tucker. "So what of it? Chester, you would probably like musicals, being a musician yourself."

"Maybe I would," said the cricket. But even the thought of music, which usually made him very happy, couldn't cheer Chester up now.

"We could go tonight," said Harry. "There's time to catch the second act of that new show that opened last week. It's just a little light review, but very enjoyable, I hear."

"Do you want to, Chester?" asked Tucker Mouse.

"Oh, I don't think so," said Chester. "Why don't you two go?"

"Is anything wrong?" asked the mouse. He suspected

The night after the movies, the Bellinis, Mario and his mother and father, went home early. Tucker Mouse and Harry Cat came over to the newsstand, as they did almost every night, to listen to Chester's adventures of the day. Of course, going to the movies was nothing new to them. They would sneak out into Times Square and dart into a theater two or three times a week. Tucker knew more secret entrances—hidden holes and loose boards—than any other mouse in New York.

And one afternoon Mario took Chester to his first movie. They sat in the balcony, and the boy put the cricket up on his shoulder so he'd have a clear view of the picture. The air conditioning in the theater was so cold Chester had to wrap himself in Mario's collar to keep from shivering. And the movie itself made him very sad. It took place in the country, which looked for all the world like Connecticut. Chester was looking so hard at the fields and trees that he forgot to follow the plot. By the end of the show, he could almost have cried for home-sickness.

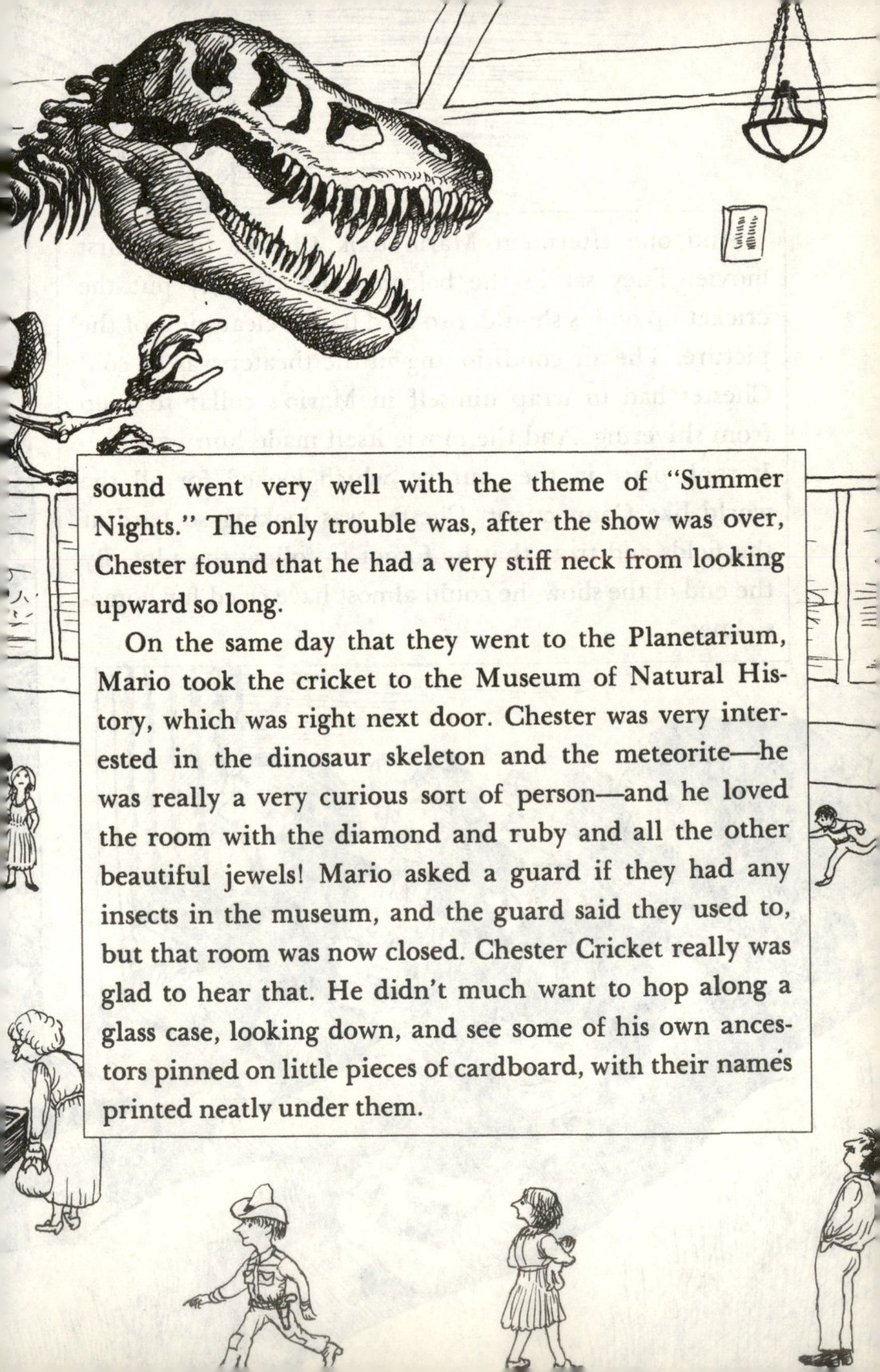

sound went very well with the theme of "Summer Nights." The only trouble was, after the show was over, Chester found that he had a very stiff neck from looking upward so long.

On the same day that they went to the Planetarium, Mario took the cricket to the Museum of Natural History, which was right next door. Chester was very interested in the dinosaur skeleton and the meteorite—he was really a very curious sort of person—and he loved the room with the diamond and ruby and all the other beautiful jewels! Mario asked a guard if they had any insects in the museum, and the guard said they used to, but that room was now closed. Chester Cricket really was glad to hear that. He didn't much want to hop along a glass case, looking down, and see some of his own ancestors pinned on little pieces of cardboard, with their names printed neatly under them.

But Chester didn't only stay in the subway station. One Sunday afternoon Mario took him to the Planetarium. Chester thought that was *awfully* interesting! Back home, his favorite pastime had been stargazing. The top of his stump made an excellent observation platform, and he loved to come out and watch the slow drift of stars across the night sky. And in the Planetarium Chester recognized the same stars. They were showing a program called "Summer Nights." But all the changes that took place in a whole summer in Connecticut, the rising and falling of the constellations, happened in just a few hours in the Planetarium. At one point, when he saw a shooting star, Chester got so excited he began to chirp. The

and introduced him to everyone who worked in the Times Square subway station. He met all the countermen from the lunchstands, the conductors on the Shuttle, the cleaning men who swept the station, and the three girls who worked in the Loft's candy store. And they all liked Chester. It somehow made them happy to think that there was a little insect from the countryside living right there in the heart of New York. He became the pet of the whole station. The countermen fed him, the conductors gave him free rides back and forth on the Shuttle, and the three girls saved him a chocolate cream candy every now and then.

Life in New York is very exciting.

It especially was thrilling for a cricket named Chester from Connecticut, who just two weeks ago had found himself in the Times Square subway station. It was there that he'd managed finally to free himself from a picnic basket. And then had been more or less adopted by two families: the Bellinis, who ran a newsstand, and a mouse and a cat named Tucker and Harry, who lived in an old abandoned drainpipe. So much happened to Chester during those first two weeks in the city that he could hardly believe he was the same country cricket who used to spend his days eating and sleeping and sunning himself on his stump in the country.

For a few days Mario Bellini, the boy who had found Chester his first night in New York, took him around

For Tom Andrews
Good friend to crickets, bees, and beets—
and me!
G.S.

An imprint of Macmillan Publishing Group, LLC

Library of Congress catalog card number: 80-20326
ISBN 978-0-312-58248-7

Originally published in the United States by Farrar Straus Giroux
Square Fish logo designed by Filomena Tuosto
First Square Fish Edition: 2009

20 19 18
mackids.com

Chester Cricket's Pigeon Ride

GEORGE SELDEN

PICTURES BY
GARTH WILLIAMS

SQUARE
FISH

FARRAR STRAUS GIROUX
NEW YORK

Chester Cricket's Pigeon Ride

Chester Cricket is homesick. When his friend Mario takes him to a sky show at the Planetarium, Chester realizes how much he misses seeing real stars at night. Happily, he finds his way out of the subway and into Times Square, where he might be able to see the sky—if he could just get past all of the bright lights. Then he meets Lulu Pigeon. Every pigeon Chester's ever known loves to eat crickets. But could Lulu turn out to be a friend? Could she fly him above the bright lights so he can see the starry night sky again?

"Williams big, breathtaking pen-and-ink drawings almost steal the show from the author."—*Publishers Weekly*

LEXILE 820L